A Summer Dream

and Other Stories

A SUMMER DREAM
AND OTHER STORIES BY STEVEN P. GREGORY

Oak Mountain Press, LLC
Birmingham, Alabama

ISBN 978-0985992835

A Summer Dream

and Other Stories

by
Steven P. Gregory

Hast thou not torn the Naiad from her flood,
The Elfin from the green grass, and from me
The summer dream beneath the tamarind tree?

—Edgar Allen Poe,
Sonnet: To Science

Oak Mountain Press
This book is dedicated to Jan, my wife and editor,

and Sam, my son and cover artist.

TABLE OF CONTENTS

THE DREAMER'S MISTRESS

During the past eighteen months, Margot Thorn had spent a total of seven days on the psychiatric floor at Our Lady of Mercy Hospital. This would make her third visit.

Dr. Vivian Kramer, her psychologist, had called Benedict at his cramped office on the third floor of the hospital, where he was reviewing charts. Benedict was chief surgical resident. "Margot is having some serious problems right now and we need you to come and help us with her admission to the unit," the psychologist had said.

Benedict had thought his wife was getting better. Nothing unusual. He couldn't remember what he'd said on the phone. He'd made it across the highway to the Psychology Clinic in five minutes.

Dr. Kramer told Benedict his wife had been abusing Vicodin for pain in her legs. Margot had been eating very little food and running 7several miles a day. She'd have to stay in the psych ward a few days to get clean.

Margot was a good runner. Last year she'd taken a second for females 30-39 in a local 10-K. Benedict had gotten her started running with the psychologist's encouragement. They'd agreed it would be therapeutic.

This time Margot didn't want to go to the ward. She made a scene. She begged. Implored. "I'm sorry. Ben," she said as soon as Benedict stepped into Dr. Kramer's office. "I won't be bad any more. Take me home. They won't let me go. I don't want to go there again. They make you watch TV. Ben, hold me."

She cried. She sat on the floor. She took off the gray felt hat Benedict had given her for her thirty-second birthday three weeks before and began to crush it. Benedict snatched it away before she could do any damage. The hat had a high crown with a blue sash around the base. The blue and gray were the colors in her eyes.

She said, "Ben if you don't take me home, I'll never make love to you again." When Benedict didn't move, Margot tried to run away. A male resident on psych rotation who happened to be standing out in the hall had to restrain her. Dr. Kramer threatened her with police, handcuffs, legal detention.

It was unpleasant. No. It was ugly. But Benedict could hardly blame her. When a patient was admitted to the psych ward they searched her luggage for sharp objects, even though, as Margot had pointed out on her first visit, there were lethal-looking hooks holding up the shower curtain. They made all the patients dress in their street clothes and take meals in the the break room, where a TV set was kept at high decibels so the geriatrics could hear their game shows.

A door of thick metal, painted beige, separated the nurses' station from the patients' room. The door had a lock the nurses could control from their station. They always had to unlock it when Benedict had visited, and they'd locked it behind him. Margot had been reading Proust the first time she'd fallen ill, and she'd taken volume three of *Remembrance of Things Past* into the ward. In the ward, she hadn't been able to read very much of Proust's narrator's sojourns by the seashore at Balbec, his interminable parties in Paris, or his walks in the woods at Combray.

This time Margot and Dr. Kramer compromised for a stay in a private room on the psychiatric floor in the unlocked wing, with a nurse on duty twenty-four hours a day. Inside the room. "Can I wear my regular clothes until bedtime?" Margot asked him when they checked in. He looked at the nurse. "I guess it's all right," she said. "But you can't go out in the hall."

Benedict stayed with her until nine, the end of visiting hours, and by then she was less reactive. Her legs hurt her some, but they'd given her aspirin. She told him she'd run ten miles that morning. He didn't ask what she'd had to eat.

She admitted she'd gotten the Vicodin without a prescription, but she refused to identify the pharmacist. He decided to let it go.

He went home and tried to study for boards. Surgical boards were in five days. Sometime after midnight, he put away the books and tried to sleep.

He slept badly. Benedict's rounds began at six a. m. About five-thirty he tracked down the first-year resident who'd been on call the night before. He worked up all candidates for reconstructive surgery, usually trauma or burn patients, himself. That was his privilege as chief resident on the service. He was considering staying two more years and getting certified in reconstructive.

The resident was reviewing charts at the nurses' station. "Anything interesting?" Benedict asked. The resident looked over the aluminum binders scattered over the counter.

"Yeah. Here. Something that might be your kind of case." He turned a page and read. "Patient admitted ten thirty-one p. m., female Caucasian, suffering what appeared to be a slicing knife wound to the left breast, causing complete severance of the nipple. Superficial treatment--cleaning and bandaging the wound--performed by resident in ER. Patient admitted for observation and consult with reconstructive surgical staff."

The resident looked up. "She's unnamed--a Miss X. Two cops brought her in. They'd found her somewhere, I guess. We couldn't get any information. Oh." He looked down at his hands. "I heard about Margot. Sorry."

Benedict shrugged. "Thanks. I think she'll be okay."

The resident nodded. "This admission is not our usual patient. A classy looking redhead. Well-dressed when she came in." He looked again at the chart. "She's in room 312. It's really too bad. Maybe we...."

Benedict grabbed the chart and was on his way down the hall before the resident could finish. "Thank you," he called over his shoulder.

Room 312 was private, one of the few on the wing, with furniture for visitors and windows down to the floor. The patient lying in the hospital bed seemed to be asleep, her face turned away.

As the door closed behind Benedict, the patient turned to face him and opened her eyes. They stared at each other for a long moment.

It was she who spoke first. "Are you all right, doctor?" Benedict shook his head as if to clear it. "Yes, I think so," he said. "A bit tired."

He walked to the side of the bed. "I'm Dr. Thorn," he said. "I understand that you've had an injury."

"Yes. "

"I'm the chief surgical resident at this hospital. May I examine the wound?" He gestured toward the dressing on her chest, visible through the thin white hospital gown.

"Of course."

Benedict helped the patient sit up and slipped the gown off her shoulders. "I'm going to have you lie flat," he said. The woman nodded, held his eyes for a moment, then lay back and shifted her gaze to the ceiling.

Benedict removed the dressing. The wound looked clean; ER had done a good job. He was almost disappointed. The procedure was relatively simple.

The woman looked at Benedict. "Will you help me?" she asked.

"Yes."

He went into the hall and came back with pads, gauze, and tape. He made a new dressing and helped her on again with the gown. "Let me explain what we'll do." He took a fiber tip pen from the pocket of his lab coat and drew a circular dotted line in ink on the inside of his own forearm. "We'll reattach like this. We can draw upon some of your own tissue for the graft. With any luck you'll be the same as ever except for a small scar. We'll schedule the procedure in a couple of days."

"Thank you, doctor," the woman said. She looked out the window for a moment, then back at Benedict. "The only thing I know about myself is that when I'm in a hospital I belong in a private room. I insisted on that last night. It's just about the first thing I remember, telling the doctors down in the emergency room that I would not under any circumstances stay in the hospital if I had to go to a ward." She took a deep breath and let it out slowly. "That's a helluva thing to know about yourself if you don't know anything else."

"I'm sure you'll remember everything soon,"
Benedict said. "Amnesia is almost always temporary."
He looked at his watch. "I'm due for rounds. I'll try to
drop by later to see how you are. "

The woman smiled. "To see if I've thought of
my name yet."

Around the surgical staff, Benedict had been
hearing disturbing rumors about boards. Devane, his
closest friend on the staff, had stopped him in the hall
and in a low voice admitted he was near panic. Benedict
tried to reassure him. But he'd heard worse from others.
Lufkin's mother was to have cancer surgery and his
father was dead and he guessed he had to be there.
Eaton Phillips went skiing on a Sunday afternoon and

almost lost a leg when she fell overboard and tangled with the prop. It looked like they'd saved the leg, but it had been close. Those were reasons, not excuses, of course, but others, like Devane, appeared about to lose their nerve.

He'd seen it before, in med school, in undergraduate science courses. Good people, people you'd had labs with, people you'd studied with, just weren't there anymore.

At 7:00 p.m. Benedict, freshly showered after two hours of emergency surgery, stopped by his office to pick up Schwartz's *Principles* and the bouquet of fresh daisies a nurse on the service had left there for Margot. He took the elevator to the fifth floor. At Margot's door he held the flowers behind his back, knocked on the door with the textbook, and pushed it open with his shoulder. The nurse, seeing him, picked up her needlepoint and walked out.

Margot was sitting up in bed wearing the clothes she'd worn yesterday, including the hat. Benedict held out the .flowers.

"Oh," Margot said. She inclined her head in a way she had of acknowledging gifts. At her best, she was impatient with cliches. "I'll take them. Thanks."

She put the flowers on the bedside table. "Well. I feel better. Thanks for saving my hat." She smiled, wary.

"Good," Benedict bent and kissed her on the lips. She got out of bed and hugged him tightly. "I'm sorry, my poor little Ben." she said to the back of his neck.

"No reason to be."

"Yes there is. I told Dr. Kramer so, too." She let him go and sat in one of the room's two upholstered chairs, both covered in rough institutional green fabric. "I'm tired of the bed. How was your day?"

He raised a hand and wagged it back and forth in appraisal. "Average."

"Would you like to stretch out on the bed to study?"

He considered. It was only a little strange, he supposed. His legs were tired. "Okay, he said."

He sat first, then leaned against the headboard with his feet dangling off each side.

"That's no good." He reached down to throw off his shoes.

"Better?" Margot asked.

"Much. "

"I have some magazines here that one of the nurses brought." She held up a copy of *House and Garden*. "I'll read of the sex lives of plants while you study."

Benedict opened his *Principles of Surgery*. Mnemonics, drill, memory. He settled back and began.

The change in Margot's behavior had begun in late summer the year Benedict's father died. Not that he attributed the one to the other. She'd lost about twenty pounds in two months, and the skin along her spine had become dry and flaked. Her body when they'd made love had felt as fragile as a child's, her hips no wider than his own.   He'd finally told her to make an appointment with Dr. Kramer. She hadn't resisted, though she'd maintained nothing was wrong. That time she'd spent three days in behavioral therapy in the psych ward at Mercy.

But the worst time had been about a year later. It was January. Her brother had died that fall, the brother just older, of complications following an automobile accident. The man, thirty-five when he died, had spent his entire adult life at home. He'd had a moderate case of scoliosis. Benedict suspected that degenerative damage to the heart and lungs caused by the twisted spine had been a contributing cause of the death. There had been no autopsy.

Margot hadn't shed a single tear then. But she began to have more and more trouble interacting with people. She decided that she had no friends, that Dr.

Kramer didn't like her, and she began to lose weight again.

"Her symptoms during this crisis are much more like those of schizophrenia," Dr. Kramer had told Benedict. She sat across from him in an armless swivel chair upholstered in black vinyl, her legs crossed, a pencil in one hand, in her office lined with dark gray soundproofing foam and psychiatry texts. "Margot has trouble matching her emotional state to the events she experiences intellectually. For example, her reaction to her brother's death."

"Um-hmm." Benedict remembered a little of one or two medical school lectures. "'Schizophrenia-- not a split personality, as the layman thinks of it, but actually a schism between emotion and mentation.'"

"I still don't believe she's diagnosable as schizophrenic."

Benedict realized Dr. Kramer was still speaking.

"I'm proceeding on the basis of her history that it's more of an atypical depression. A couple of articles in the literature mention schizoid-like symptoms in some of these patients. Anorexics tend to have these atypical depressions."

"A couple of articles?"

"I know it doesn't sound like much to go on." She smiled as if in apology. "Margot is not a typical patient. For one thing, she's much brighter than most." She uncrossed her legs, the swish of nylon making Benedict aware of her femaleness. "I want to try some drug therapy while she's in the hospital where we can observe her closely. The resident on psychiatry can write the orders for me."

They'd tried nearly everything in the drug store. One problem was that Margot's system did not tolerate the psychoactive agents well. Haldol slurred her speech; Mellaril blew her pupils wide and blurred her vision. They finally settled on three milligrams of Stelazine and one hundred fifty milligrams of Ludiomil daily.

The drugs lifted her spirits; she smiled more often, and after she was out of the hospital they started going out more, to a restaurant, to an occasional party. The Stelazine seemed at least to stitch her emotional self loosely to her rational side.

But she still wasn't quite the same as when he'd met her, and she rarely laughed aloud.

Benedict jerked and opened his eyes. For a moment he couldn't think where he was. Then he remembered. He'd fallen asleep studying in his wife's hospital bed. He'd been dreaming, and for a moment that was all he knew, but then the dream returned to him in one piece as though he'd seen an entire feature-length film compressed into one moment.

In the dream he'd been carrying about in the pocket of his clinic coat a human female nipple, sliced, he was certain, from the chest of the woman with no name in room 312.

The dream was in color; his dreams were usually black and white. The nipple had seemed still alive, though when his dreaming self had taken it out of the pocket, with it had come a bent paper clip, a crumbling aspirin, and a few balls of cotton fuzz.   The hospital room door opening stopped him. A nurse with short blond hair and an efficient smile said, "It's 9:20, Doc. You really should be going now."

"Oh. Yes, all right. Thank you," Benedict said. "I'll be right out." He swung off the bed, put on his shoes, and crossed the room to his wife. They kissed.

"Good night, sweetheart," he said to her. "See you tomorrow. Get some sleep."

Margot yawned. "Good night, husband," she said.

The night was crisp and cool, the sky clear. Benedict walked the ten blocks home at a pace just short of a jog. He breathed deeply and tried to relax. He felt as though his nerve fibers were slowly being stripped away from muscle and bone. Relax. Lying on the hospital bed, he'd done nothing but dream. In the apartment, Benedict told himself that the thing to do was to stay busy and not think. He scanned the newspaper and then settled down to study. He'd be damned if he'd let the others put him off this thing. He'd study, and he'd pass.

Around 1:30 in the morning Benedict realized he'd read over the same page four times. Still he didn't feel sleepy.

He went upstairs to the bathroom, took off his clothes and washed his face. In a drawer beside the vanity he moved things around until he found a single ten-milligram Ambien tablet in its sample package of foil and plastic. He poured water in a bathroom glass, dissolved the tablet, and drank off the bitter solution in one swallow. Thirty seconds after his head contacted the pillow, he was asleep.

During the next day, two more senior residents, grave as sophomores, came to Benedict with tales of woe and fear.

Cooper, the academic hotshot from Yale, the resident whose mind Benedict envied a little, had almost lost an eye playing racquetball and so of course he couldn't study.

Celeste Miller, the black woman from Arkansas who'd graduated summa cum laude from Stanford, had a death in her family and might even have to leave surgery for a general practice in rural south Arkansas.

And that morning, Benedict had gotten out of bed with his own doubts. He didn't seem to have the time just now that he needed to devote to study.

Just before lunch Benedict caught Dr. Kramer as she was leaving her office across the street from the hospital and asked if he could see her for a moment. They stepped into a conference room.

"I'm having trouble concentrating on these boards coming up," he said. "I needed to tell someone. You know, some of the senior residents are suddenly falling ill or just plain talking about waiting until next year, taking an extra year."

"Do you think it's that hard to pass?"

Benedict rubbed the back of his neck. "Well -- no. Intellectually, I know it can't be. The surgical attendings say it's a piece of cake. But emotionally, psychologically, you start after so many years, some people begin to break, I guess."

"But not you."

He shook his head. "It's just overload. I'll survive."

"Of course you will."

"Thanks for listening, though."

That evening Benedict couldn't get to his wife's room before eight. He convinced the nurses before he went in to let him stay past visiting hours. This time Margo was wearing a hospital gown. "I just couldn't keep the same dress on for several days, could I?" she said as he entered the room. She sat in one of the chairs, one leg curled under.

"No," he said.

"So I decided to just go ahead and be sick. Maybe I'll get well sooner." She stood, took his face between her palms, and studied his eyes. Then she kissed him. Her hair was clean and brushed and pulled back from her face with clips. "You look tired," she said. "You can have the bed again if you want."

"Okay," Benedict said.

For an hour Benedict was able to work more intensely than he had in days. Absorbed, he hardly glanced up when Margot got up from her chair, pushed the door to the hall firmly closed, and went into the bathroom. In two minutes the light from the bathroom made him look up and, naked, warm, and perfumed, Margot was already getting into bed with him.

Tossing his books onto the floor, she began to cover his face in tiny damp kisses. His clothes fell away as if a powerful wind had blown through the room, and soon she had forced matters along until she was astride and moving for them.

Margot had taut firm breasts with brown nut-like nipples, but as he looked at her his mind flashed to the pink nipple in his dream.

When the sex was over, Benedict turned on his side and fell headlong toward sleep.

Benedict's left leg jerked convulsively and then the dream began. The dream seemed to last for hours, repeating over and over. He sometimes glimpsed the shadowy blond silhouette of a woman. This time in part of the dream he saw his hand, holding his scalpel, the fingers guiding it in a precise incision around the border of the areola.

Benedict awoke with a vague sense of unease. The overhead light in the room was still on, but for a moment he wasn't sure where he was. Then he remembered. He looked down at the two naked bodies on the bed, one hairy and blunt, the other sleek and hairless except for V at the pubis, a body like a whippet's, quadriceps that bulged slightly in the belly of the muscle.

He leaned over to check the time on his wife's travel alarm on the bedside table. It was 10:35 p.m.

When he turned back, the nurse with short blond hair was standing in the doorway, determinedly unshockable, her mouth beginning now to close. She looked him right in the eye. "Time to go," she said.

Benedict sat and pulled the sheet over his genitals as Margot woke up. "Okay," he said to the nurse. "Give me five minutes to get dressed."

For the next couple of days, Benedict divided his time between his textbooks, surgery, Margot, and the patient in room 312. He was on call on Wednesday, the day Dr. Kramer allowed his wife to return home. She and the psych resident had decided Margot hadn't

reached a dependency status with the Vicodin.

Benedict pulled a thirty-six hour stretch without

spending a moment at home, eating hospital food and

sleeping a few hours on a couch in the resident's lounge.

The woman in 312 was recovering quickly, the nipple

graft almost healed. He still did not know her name.

A couple more residents dropped by to say they

were postponing boards. Few were left.

On Friday morning Benedict awoke in the

apartment at six. He had slept through the night with

no dreams.

Margot made him a light breakfast. He

showered, shaved, dressed and reported at eight to a

classroom in the medical sciences building at the

University.

The proctor was the only other person there. Thirty minutes into the allotted time, Devane appeared at the door and motioned to the proctor. They went into the hall. After five minutes the proctor returned alone.

Benedict was the only survivor. He took less than the permissible time for the exam. The proctor promised the results in a week.

He passed.

###

REAL ESTATE

It started on Sunday. The Andersons slept late. Ralph puttered about between the bedroom and bathroom, shaving, doing his daily fifty sit-ups and twenty-five push-ups, while Millie began breakfast. The maid had Sundays off.

After his calisthenics Ralph showered; afterwards, he stood before the full-length mirror in the dressing room admiring his chiseled midsection, his graying, handsome profile, when Millie burst in, startling him into dropping his towel. "Millie," he said, chagrined. "You could knock or something."

"Sorry. I didn't expect to find the Nude Mr. Universe in my dressing room."

Ralph winced. "I just got out of the shower. Breakfast ready?"

"Almost." She started to go but hung back.

"What is it? Anything wrong? Didn't burn the toast again, did you?"

"Hah. I don't know. It's probably silly. Probably it's nothing. I'm probably just being a silly woman."

"But. . . ."

"Well, there's this car. It's parked out front, some little silver car. Japanese I think. There's a driver in it, but I couldn't see him very well. A young man, it looked like."

Ralph opened a dresser drawer and selected a pair of blue-striped boxer shorts. "Is it parked on our side of the street?"

"What? No. On the other side," Millie said. "Probably I'm just being a worrier. Let me go put breakfast on the table."

"Why don't you do that? Leave a man to dress in peace." He looked at her and spoke more softly. "I'll be down in a minute."

Ralph came to the breakfast room in knit golf pants, Polo shirt, and slippers. He drew a cup of coffee from the Capresso machine, sat down and began buttering a slice of toast.

Millie came in carrying a bowl of scrambled eggs and sat down across from Ralph. "He's still there," she said.

Ralph sipped his coffee. "Maybe he wants to buy the house," he finally offered.

"He has an odd way of going about it."

"He's studying it," Ralph added.

Millie cradled a cup of coffee in both hands and raised her eyebrows.

"That's it." Ralph began to warm to the notion. "He wants to buy the place and he's going to sit out there and intimidate us into selling. Whether we want to or not. These real estate agents," he added, considering the implications of his theory. "They'll do anything to make a deal these days. I know 'em." He virtually chortled, convinced now that he was right. "I was talking to Frank Lawson just last week and I told him the profit motive is fine, and times are hard, but my God. . . ." He broke off and shook his head sharply.

"I'm sure you're right, honey. The house isn't for sale, though."

"Of course not."

"It does beat the stock market for conversation these days."

That remark met with a frown from Ralph which Millie ignored. Ralph was a stockbroker. Despite a strong rally off the lows, business had not been good since 2009. Individual investors seemed permanently spooked.

"So I'll just stop worrying." Millie took a dainty bite of egg. "Who' s in the foursome today?"

Ralph played a round of golf at the country club every Sunday morning.

"I don't know. Frank Lawson for sure. That new neurosurgeon, what's his name? The Hungarian Jew?"

"Dr. Weiser?"

"Right. Weiser. And some accountant at Tri States Paper. Friend of Frank's.

Millie came around the table to kiss her husband lightly on the mouth. "Better finish your coffee and get going, honey. Don't want to keep the boys waiting."

Ralph backed his little Mercedes down the drive and into Laurel Street. As casually as possible, he let his glance fall on the small car. The driver's face was partly obscured by tinted windows, and he was turned away from Ralph, apparently studying something spread on the seat. As he drove by, Ralph stared. The young man looked up and Ralph turned away immediately, but he had seen that the man was young, perhaps in his middle twenties, and that he wore a thin, well-groomed beard. As he turned onto Clubhouse Road, Ralph noted that the young man had turned back to whatever he was studying.

The clubhouse was only a half mile away. Ralph parked beside Frank Lawson's Volvo. The other members of the foursome were already out on the putting green behind the clubhouse. Ralph put his clubs in the cart beside theirs and walked over to the green. The bentgrass was still lightly frosted with dew. "Morning, gentlemen," he said.

The fourth hole of the Rolling Hills Country Club golf course, 433 yards, par four, dogleg left, ran within fifty yards of Laurel. Ralph played his second shot and stood at the edge of the fairway, his back to the others, gazing toward his house. Where the little car had been parked, the street was partially obscured by trees, but Ralph thought he could make out a chrome fender through the foliage.

"Not that anxious to get home to Millie, are you, Ralph?" Frank Lawson said at his elbow.

"What? Uhh---nah."

"None of us are newlyweds anymore, after all. You know," he went on, as Ralph's gaze didn't change direction, "that's a great home you and Millie have.

Really beautiful. It's one of the few really unique homes in this town. I've

told Polly before, you know, that you guys have the best looking house in Tuscaloosa. You wouldn't consider selling it, would you?"

Ralph spun around. "No. Of course not. What gave you that idea?"

Frank Lawson raised his arms and shoulders in an exaggerated shrug. "It's my business, Ralph. Just asking."

"Well, it's not for sale," Ralph muttered, embarrassed by his reaction.

"Okay, buddy. Let's play golf."

After the round, Ralph sat in the club sauna for twenty minutes, took a long hot shower, dried, and dressed. He moved slowly out to his car. He felt great except that every step felt like he was plodding through wet concrete. Stayed in the sauna too long, he told himself. Have to watch that. Shouldn't follow the sauna with a hot shower, anyway. Made you weak as water.

When Ralph turned into his street, the little silver car was gone. He hesitated for a moment, then whipped the Mercedes into the spot where the young man had been parked. He shut off the engine and sat still, his hands gripping the steering wheel.

He wondered what his house had looked like to the young man, to someone who'd never seen it before. Perhaps, viewing the house from this new perspective, he could hit upon a stranger's reason for parking here.

He no longer felt sure of the rationale he'd developed that morning. Millie. . . .no. Best to push that thought as far away as possible.

Experimentally, he glanced at his house out of the corner of his eye. All he saw were patches of white interrupted by green. His peripheral vision had never been much. He looked straight ahead again and reached to roll down the window. You're a young real estate agent, a real sharpie, sent out to appraise the Andersons' place, he told himself. In this guise, Ralph turned and looked directly at the house across the street.

Frank Lawson was right, he realized. 1000 Laurel Street was gorgeous. The architect Ralph and Millie had commissioned to design a home just for this site had called the concept "Gothic contemporary." Built on three levels, the house seemed much smaller than it was;

the inherent compactness of its hexagonal shape belied the size of the rooms. The glass-walled formal dining room jutting out to the right seemed to float weightless behind the library tower. It had cost a million dollars to build twelve years ago. What was it worth now, even in this market? A million and a half? More?

Ralph shook his head sharply to clear it of this madness. The house wasn't for sale at any price. Millie expected to live there the rest of her life. He started the Mercedes and eased across to the driveway.

At the office next morning Ralph made his early round of calls to his active customers, then sat back at nine to watch the ticker. Trading was slow for the first hour. At ten he found himself drumming his fingers on his desk and he could stand it no longer. He picked up the phone.

"Frank, buddy," he began when Frank Lawson came on the line. "How's real estate today?"

"Could not be better, Ralph. Seriously. If it keeps on like this I'm gonna be looking for more agents."

Ralph smiled to himself. "Sure you are. With interest rates this low, you should have lines forming outside your door. But you don't."

"That's the problem you stockbrokers have, Ralph. You believe everything you read in the *Wall Street Journal*."

Ralph leaned back and smoothed a hand over his hair. "And nothing we read in the *New York Times*. So tell me, do you have a line of buyers forming at your door? One day real estate looks like a bargain, the next I read that the only buyers are national syndicators buying short sales and foreclosures to place in public partnerships and rent. I've thought about buying some apartments in town, but then I read an article suggesting football might be banned because of head injuries. I don't need to tell you what that would do to real estate in this town."

"Cross yourself three times when you speak of football, my friend."

Ralph nodded. The University had won two championships in the last five years, and this coach didn't have to walk on water. He flew above it. Football sustained the school, the city, and half the state. "So tell me about real estate. On that subject, I don't know whether to wind my ass or scratch my wristwatch."

"Low interest rates may be hurting bond sales, but housing is hot. You'd be surprised, for instance, just how many people are buying homes for cash."

"Cash?"

"Three, four, five hundred thousand, even a million dollars. Numbers don't mean a thing. You know Indian Shores, that neighborhood?"

"Sure."

"Had a house listed two weeks, an estate really, pool, tennis court, stable, secluded five acres on the lake. Get the picture?"

Ralph was silent.

"Anyway, it's listed two weeks. Two million bucks, right? Last week, a guy comes in wearing a ski sweater and corduroy jacket, pipe sticking out of his pocket, trim little beard. I figure him for a University prof. He sits down."

"Did you say beard?"

"What? Yeah. So? Everybody's wearing a beard these days. Bernanke, Paul Krugman. I'm about to talk Polly into me giving one a try."

"How old?" Ralph was leaning forward now, his elbows on the desk.

"What?"

Ralph forced a casual tone. "Young guy, old, what?"

"I don't know, what's the difference? Twenty-eight, twenty-nine, maybe."

Ralph exhaled into the phone. "Shit," he said.

"What was that?"

"Nothing." Ralph closed his eyes. "Go ahead."

"Well, it's not a big deal or anything, Christ, it's not the sale of the century, but this guy and I talk for a minute and suddenly he's asking about the Indian Shores house. And then he says, all of a sudden but like he's known all along, 'I

want that house' he says.

"It's two million they're asking, I say."

"Right," he says, and then he pulls out this certified check and I nearly drop my socks. I mean, I figured this guy for a three-bedroom ranch. And get this, Ralph." He paused.

"Yeah?"

"This check is for two million fifty-thousand dollars. Drawn on First National. He sort of smiles, says, 'Will that cover closing costs?' Geez. You and I both see lots of money, but that really blew me away."

There was a short silence.

"So it's like that all the time, huh?" Ralph ventured.

"Well, not exactly like that, but it has been--uh--active."

One of Ralph's customers walked in the front door of the office and Ralph waved. "I've gotta go, Frank, but I really enjoyed our talk. We're all going to have to get together sometime soon for dinner or something. I'll talk to Millie. Check with you later, Frank."

"Sure, Ralph. Ciao." Ralph stared at the handset in surprise for a moment before he dropped it back in its cradle.

At home Ralph found Millie reading in the library. "Millie, something you won't believe. . . ."

"You're home early," she said. "He's been out there today."

Ralph set his briefcase by the door and walked over to kiss his wife. "Same guy?"

"Of course. Who else? He was there in the same spot from nine to two. At nine forty-five I called the police, but they said there was nothing they could do. Unless he really did something besides just sit in his car. I did see a patrol car pass, but it didn't stop."

"Let me tell you what I found out. It'll amaze you," Ralph said.

"Three things. First, the local real estate market is hotter than I knew. Frank Lawson says. . . ."

"You spoke with Frank Lawson?"

"Yeah. He says he may take on more agents, houses are so hot. Second, he's taken to saying things like 'Ciao' at the end of phone conversations."

"Ciao?"

"You know, it' s--uh--Italian for goodbye or whatever. Back in the late nineties stockbrokers used to say it, sometimes. Guys making a fortune on the dotcoms. Of course, later most of them lost those fortunes and then some in the NASDAQ crash."

"Ralph, what on earth has that to do with. . . ."

"Everything, honey, everything. Only very, very, confident businessmen start sprinkling foreign phrases into telephone conversations. And third. . . ." He paused and looked into Millie's eyes. "Our man has bought a house from Frank." He waited for this last to register. When it didn't, he pressed on. "The guy you called the police about? Young man, trim beard? He bought a two million dollar estate out on Indian Lake through Frank just a couple of weeks ago."

"You're sure it was. . . ."

"Positive. How many people just like that are going around looking for houses?"

Millie nodded slowly. "And now he's looking at ours. But why? A young man like that? Who could he be?"

"Not who he is. Whom he represents. I think it's either Tri-States Paper or maybe Shafer Iron buying up some executive homes for some reason. Maybe expansion. I'm inclined to think maybe Tri-States. It sounds like the hush-hush sort of game they like to play. I've heard they may be launching a bid for Southern Paper and moving the combined headquarters here."

"That accountant you played golf with? The friend of Frank's? Did he mention anything?"

"Not a word. You wouldn't have known where he worked. They're playing it crafty and Frank's definitely in on the deal."

Millie stood up. "Let me show you what I've done today." She walked to her desk beside one of the room's floor-to-ceiling windows and came back with three books. "I checked out some books. "

Ralph read the titles aloud. "Sell Your Own House. Be Your Own Real-Estate Agent. How to Make a Million Dollars in Real Estate."

He looked up. "Decided to go back to work?"

Millie smiled, "Maybe." She tapped the edge of the coffee table with a finger. "And I'd like to start right here."

Ralph picked up the three volumes and flipped through the first few pages. "These are old books, you know. Printed back when real estate was booming in the eighties. We're post-crash now. Despite Frank Lawson's line of schmooze and maybe some local, temporary issues based on demand for a certain kind of house, real estate nationwide is hardly booming. Hanging on by its fingernails, more like."

"Old books, maybe, but still filled with good advice, Ralph. Like you."

Ralph smiled. "You'd really sell our house?"

In answer Millie stood and walked to the window. After a silence she said, "I talked with Martha Schotts this morning. You know she's started selling real estate. Ralph," she whirled to face her husband, "Martha says she could sell our house in a minute for a million and a half. Ralph, we could get a place on the lake." She took a step toward him. "What do you say?"

Ralph gave her a hapless grin. "What can I say? Do it."

Tuesday was another slow day in the markets. Gold was stuck in a tight trading range and it looked as though if they ever got their act together the Greeks would pull out of the euro. Ralph wanted to short the euro, but his firm, a traditional stock and bond house, didn't trade futures. Around one Ralph's secretary buzzed him to say that Frank Lawson was on the line. Ralph tapped in Frank's name and account number on his computer terminal and a digest of his account flashed on the display screen. Ralph pushed Frank's line and spoke. "Frank? How are you today?"!

"Never mind that, you sneaky bastard."

"What?"

"I saw your FSBO ad on the web. 'Custom designed house on golf course for sale by owner.' You could have let me know."

"Oh, are you still interested, Frank? We would have listed with you of course, but Millie wants to try her hand at selling first. I think she may be interested in going for her real estate license. Say, since you called, you know you ought to consider acquiring some more Walmart now. That Mexican bribery story has been blown way out of proportion. You know the liberal media hate Walmart. The stock is cheap."

"'Cheap.' Crap. It's twelve bucks below where I bought it, I know that. Listen, Polly and I might be interested in looking at your house with a buyer's eyes if we're still invited."

"Sure, come on out anytime. Tonight if you want to. So you're not interested in doing business today, huh?

"All the business I can handle right here. See you later, Ralph."

"Ciao, Frank."

Around three-fifteen the market had closed down two points on light volume and Ralph decided to call it a day. Pulling into Laurel he saw with an unexpected sense of alarm that the bearded young man was once again in place behind the wheel of his small silver car.

Inside, Millie was seated in a straight chair pulled up at an angle near the library window. The telephone was on the floor beside her chair. As Ralph entered the room she was holding a pair of binoculars to her eyes.

"Any calls?"

Millie spun around. "Ralph! You startled me." She checked her watch. "You're home early, aren't you?"

Ralph tossed his coat across a chair and loosened his tie. "Um-hmm. Any calls yet?"

"No. I guess it's early. That young man's been out there, though. "

"I talked to Frank. They might come by tonight to look at the place."

Ralph took the binoculars from his wife's hand and looked through them, adjusting the focusing knobs until he could see the young man as though from ten feet away. "Can you see what he's doing through these things?"

"He's worked at something there in the car all day. Drawing or something on a legal pad. I couldn't make out what."

"Doodling, probably." Ralph considered. "Might be drawing the house though. Or figuring estimates. I can't tell either." He brought the binoculars down. "He's been there all day?"

"Honey, he even ate his lunch there. At noon he took out a sandwich wrapped in foil and proceeded to have his lunch right there in his car."

"Geez." Ralph shook his head. "He's persistent, whatever his purpose is." He raised his arms and looked again out the window through the binoculars. "Hey,

Millie," he said. "Something's happening. He's getting out of the car."

"Is he. . . which way's he going? He's coming this way, isn't he?"

Ralph nodded, sliding the knot of his tie tight once again. "He's crossing the street." He picked up his coat. "I'll get the door. Remember, act nonchalant. We're in no hurry to sell."

"That way we keep the price high."

Ralph nodded a sharp yes. "I'll go to the door. You can come down after he's inside."

"Oh, I'm excited. I just can't help it. I am excited." Millie stood on her toes for a moment, her eyes widening, gazing at Ralph. "This is going to be great."

Ralph was trying hard to suppress a wide grin. "That's it. Confidence. Remember, though, not too excited. We're not really anxious. . . ."

The doorbell froze both the Andersons for an instant. Millie recovered first. She reached out to squeeze her husband's fingers. "Confidence, honey," she whispered.

Ralph took a deep breath. "Right." He paused at the door. "Well, this is it," he said, and started downstairs.

###

THE BLUE VOLVO

They'd argued briefly about what to do after the lawyer, Harris, died in their living room.

The lawyer had been sitting across from them in a wing chair with salmon and beige stripes that matched the curtains Becky had ordered after she had moved into the house with Martin and redecorated. The lawyer wore steel-rimmed glasses tinted a light grey; his hair was dark and clipped short. He had heavy brows that made him look like he was scowling. His eyes were brown and liquid.

Harris had been listening to them talk about incorporating the newsletter business and making new wills, asking questions, making notes on a yellow legal pad. Suddenly, without a word, but looking at them almost in apology, he'd pitched over onto the floor.

Martin, who'd taken CPR, felt for a pulse and then pumped on the lawyers's chest. She'd wanted to dial 911 but Martin wouldn't hear of it.

"They'd investigate," he'd said, his fingers locked across the lawyer's chest.

"So what? We haven't done anything. For God's sake, Martin, we have to call. Investigate? I'm a secretary. You're retired from the University. We have to call." But she'd made no move for the phone.

Martin looked up, his hands still rhythmically

compressing the rib cage. "The calls we've been getting. You know they're just looking for a chance to go after people like us. You know."

The calls had been coming since the day she'd moved in. They'd been calling for "Marty" for about six months before. They'd call when he wasn't there:

"Is Marty there?"

"No, Marty's not here right now. Could I take a message?"

"Is this Becky?"

"This is Rebecca. Who's calling? Do I know you? Are you a friend of Martin's?"

"This is Sam, Becky. Is ol' Marty still selling guns?"

"No. Martin has never sold guns. He publishes a newsletter about guns. He doesn't sell them."

"Oh. Okay, Becky. Talk to you later."

The calls had started about the time the latest bill to ban assault weapons had been introduced in Congress. The caller had used Caller ID Block.

When the first call came, Rebecca had told Martin about it in an offhand way.

He'd just nodded. "The feds," he'd said.

But the lawyer never started breathing and Martin could never find a pulse. After a while he'd sat back on his heels, shaking the tension out of his arms. "No use," he said.

She was silent for a moment. Then she said, "At

least let's call his wife now."

"She'd call the paramedics. She'd want to know why we didn't call the paramedics."

"We should call the paramedics. We can still call. We should already have called. I'm going to call now."

Kneeling by the dead lawyer's body, Martin reached up to grasp her wrist gently. "We already talked about this, Rebecca. We aren't calling anyone," he said.

"You're hurting me," she said, though he was not.

"I'm sorry," he said. "But no phone calls. We agreed. No phone calls. Okay?" He released his grasp tentatively.

Abruptly Rebecca sat down on the floor beside him. "It's too late now, anyway," she said. "They could establish the time of death. They'd want to know why we didn't call. It's too late to call." A great gasping sob escaped from the back of her throat. "Shit."

"Well, I'm not sure time of death determinations are that precise," Martin said. "But we have to do what we planned. We have to be strong, Rebecca."

She sobbed again but nodded. "Okay. Okay. Get his keys."

Martin dragged the body into the den. The dead lawyer had on khaki pants and a blue oxford cloth shirt. One foot was shod with a Brooks running shoe; the other with a white athletic sock. The crutches the lawyer had brought with him were lying beside the body. He'd broken a toe, he'd explained; a household accident.

The lawyer had driven up in a blue Volvo station wagon. He was married to one of her boss's patients and he was the only lawyer she knew. She'd met him when he brought their two-year-old to wait for the boy's mother during a session with Dr. Thweatt. He was maybe thirty-five and a jogger. He wasn't the kind of guy you'd expect to die in your living room.

She put on a pair of plastic examination gloves out of the box they'd gotten from the hospital when Martin had his deviated septum repaired. The door of the Volvo was locked. The man had been careful. The key wouldn't turn in the lock. She pulled it out and looked at it. It was the right key, "VOLVO" in block letters on the black plastic handle. On the key ring was a tan leather oval with "I LOVE DADDY" stitched in red.

She turned the key over and tried it again. The key turned and she got in and started the engine. The car was full of the two-year-old's toys and torn pages of children's books. There was a car seat belted down in the middle of the back seat.

She drove the Volvo across the end of the driveway, onto the grass and dirt in the back yard, and around to the back of the house. She stopped near the brick patio and got out. She looked around. The back yard was completely encircled by trees and shrubbery. She could see no one.

Martin opened the sliding glass door that separated the den from the patio. "Get the back door open," he said.

She opened the heavy back door of the wagon. There was plenty of room. Room for several bodies. The ultimate yuppie hearse: a blue Volvo station wagon. Functional. Sensible. Safe.

"Help me drag him to the car," Martin said.

The lawyer had looked thin but he was

surprisingly heavy. It took them five minutes to drag the body to the back of the Volvo and heave it in. Rebecca went back and got the crutches, threw them in the back of the wagon. They stuck over the back of the back seat.

"I'll get the tarp," Martin said. He went into the garage.

When Martin returned with the heavy gray canvas tarpaulin they used when they went camping, Rebecca said, "It won't work, Martin."

"Sure it will," Martin said. "I'll wrap the tarp around him. "We'll drive out and then leave the car. Someone will find it. We'll. . . ."

"That's not what I mean. How are we going to put him behind the wheel? Out on the highway? Someone will see us."

"No they won't. I know a place. Don't worry. Stay with me now. It'll be okay."

Martin spread the tarp over the body and slammed the rear door. Martin pulled on a pair of the exam gloves and got in the Volvo; she walked across the front yard and got into her muddy green Bronco parked at the curb.

She'd met Martin three years ago. She'd been working for Dr. Thweatt for fifteen years, since Ryan divorced her. Her only son was grown and going to college in the South. She'd spent ten years in analysis with a colleague of Dr. Thweatt's. Her file said she was dysthymic with paranoid tendencies. She didn't go to bars. She didn't go to church. She'd been lonely.

Martin Dyess had responded to her Heartlines ad in the *The Birmingham News*: 45-year-old DWF, blonde, pretty, certifiably sane, seeks SWM 40-60, non-smoker, no drugs, for serious relationship.

Martin had lost his wife to cancer the year before. He worked in the mechanical engineering department at the University as a technician. He was a year away from retirement when they'd met.

She'd had trouble getting to know Martin. He was a quiet man. He had a sense of humor she supposed would be called "dry." He was a balding man with bifocals and a dark beard so heavy he often shaved twice a day, a man of not quite average height, a man who walked with a slight limp, the result of a bone cyst which had developed in his ankle when he was nineteen.

They'd been dating a few months before he'd told her what he wanted to do after he retired. His wife had left him a small newsletter called *Military Rifle Journal*. The newsletter had been started by her first husband, who had passed it on to her when he died. She'd kept it going for ten years. It had been her first husband's hobby, a hobby that managed to support itself.

Martin had never seen a military rifle before he married Ruth. The closest he'd come to military service was being declared 4F for the Vietnam War draft. But Ruth had a large collection of twentieth-century military weapons she'd inherited from her husband.

Soon, Martin had begun collecting, too. He'd acquired a class 1 federal firearms license, which allowed him to buy and sell automatic weapons to other collectors and dealers. He'd given up the class 1 license before Ruth died. He'd kept a couple of M-16's, an Uzi, and three 1960's vintage Chinese AK-47's, never fired, still packed with assembly instructions. You were as likely to see a semi-automatic pistol on an end table in his living room as a book or a copy of *Sports Illustrated*.

Rebecca followed Martin, driving the lawyer's Volvo, down the street and out of the subdivision. It was a late summer Saturday afternoon. Kids were riding bikes and running through the water sprayed from sprinklers; husbands, returning home from golf, were taking their clubs out of the trunks of BMW's and Honda's and putting them in the garage.

They drove out of the subdivision, past the Green Valley Country Club, took Highway 42 south five miles and exited onto a county road Rebecca had never seen.

Rebecca followed the blue Volvo with its lifeless cargo five miles east on the county road. From the vantage point of the front seat of the Bronco she could just see into the rear of the station wagon, where the cargo rolled slightly left or right under the tarpaulin with each curve. Finally, Martin slowed and turned on his blinker. They turned off the road onto a dirt track that was wide and graveled at the turn-off but narrowed quickly into two ruts and disappeared into the trees.

A quarter of a mile in, the dirt track veered sharply to the right around a broad oak tree. There was a clear space under the tree. Martin guided the Volvo into the clear space. Rebecca stopped the Bronco in the track on the other side of the tree. She sat in the car as

Martin got out of the Volvo and walked back to the Bronco.

"Come on," he said. "Help me move him behind the wheel. We have to carry him this time."

She took a deep breath and shook her head, but she got out of the Bronco and followed Martin. He opened the rear door of the station wagon, pulled the tarpaulin off the body and laid it aside on the deep, dry sage grass that grew in clumps under the oak.

They staggered under the weight of the body up to the driver's door and, pushing and pulling, wedged the body into the driver's seat. Sweat pooled in Rebecca's eyebrows.

The head slumped over on the steering wheel. Martin reached across the body and snapped the seat belt into place. He closed the door. They walked back toward the Bronco, Martin stooping to pick up the tarpaulin on the way. He opened the Bronco's rear door, stuffed in the tarpaulin, and got in on the passenger's side.

Neither of them said anything until they had returned to the house.

"I just want a cool shower," Rebecca said in the foyer.

"Yeah. It's a hot day," Martin said.

When she got out of the shower Martin was sitting in the middle of their bed cleaning a Luger. "Mrs. Harris called," he said.

"What did you tell her?"

"Told her you were in the shower and you'd call back."

"What did you tell her about her husband?"

"That he left half an hour ago."

"Okay."

Becky made a cup of tea and sat in the living room looking out the window. She thought briefly about calling Dr. Thweatt and asking him for advice. Dr. Thweatt was calm and practical, for a psychiatrist. He'd have an answer, but she was pretty sure it would not be the answer Martin wanted.

Becky finished her tea and went into the kitchen to empty the dishwasher. Martin had finished cleaning the Luger and had started disassembling an AK-47. Martin wore thin latex disposable gloves to clean weapons; he said the cleaning fluid irritated his skin. He hadn't looked up as she walked by the bedroom.

Outside, a blue and white police car, moving

slowly, eased up to the curb in front of the house and

stopped. Becky watched as the officer inside the car

spoke on his radio and then opened the door of the

cruiser. The policeman was short, maybe five-eight, and

stocky, with a military crewcut. Speaking into a

microphone clipped to his shirt collar, he was still talking

to someone, a dispatcher, she guessed, as he walked up

to the front door. Becky went into the living room and

opened the door after the officer rang the bell.

"Mrs. Miller?" the officer said.

"Yes," Becky answered.

"I'm sorry to disturb you, ma'am, but we're

looking for someone whose wife reported him missing.

A lawyer named Harris? His wife tells us he had an appointment with you today?"

"Yes," said Becky. "We did have an appointment with him but he left a few hours ago."

"Were you and your husband both at home when Harris was here?"

"We were both here, yes, sir."

"Do you mind if I come in and ask you and your husband a few more questions?"

"No, not at all, officer. Come in." She turned aside to open the door wider and spoke over her shoulder to Martin as the officer stepped past her. "Martin? An officer is here about that lawyer and wants to ask a few questions. Are you busy?" She closed the door behind the policeman and turned to show him to a chair.

Martin stepped through the doorway into the hall leading out of the living room. Becky saw that he held the Luger he'd been cleaning in both hands stretched out in front of him. She was about to say, "Martin, what are you doing?" when the gun popped loudly twice and the police officer fell to the floor between her and the rocking chair she had pointed him toward.

Into the deafening silence after the gunshots, Becky began to cry. "Martin, what have you done?" she asked.

"Shut up," he said. "What does it look like I've done? There was no other way out for us. Once that police car rolled up in front of the house, our destiny was written."

Martin had never spoken in this way to Becky before. She'd stopped crying not because of what he'd said but out of shock that he would speak to her in that manner. "Isn't that why we moved the lawyer's body?" she said. "So we would be okay if this happened?"

Martin shook his head. "We were never going to be okay. Now, look, we're going to have to move this body too. We've already gotten rid of one body today. What's another? After that we're taking the cash and our passports out of the safe and flying to Mexico. I know a guy down there, in Guadalajara. We'll be fine once we cross the border."

"Martin, that's insane. We won't make it out of Alabama."

"We will. You'll see. We'll get someone to fly us in a small plane. For a couple thousand they won't ask questions. Pack a bag. We'll leave after we get rid of the body."

They rolled the body onto a tarpaulin. There was surprisingly little blood. "Hollow points," Martin said. "Low muzzle velocity. No exit wounds."

They wrapped the tarp around the body like a shroud, dragged it out to the garage, and heaved it into the trunk of Becky's Toyota. Becky packed some clothes and personal items in a couple of suitcases while Martin opened the safe and placed their cash and a few gold coins in a briefcase.

Martin placed her suitcase in the back seat of her Camry and told her he would drive his pickup and that she could follow him back to the place where they'd driven the lawyer's Volvo. He handed her the Luger and told her to place it under her seat. Becky noticed he still wore the gloves.

"We'll take the gun out to the site. With any luck the police may conclude the lawyer killed the police officer and then collapsed from a heart attack," Martin said.

Becky wasn't sure, but she got into the Camry and followed Martin out of the subdivision and back down the roads they taken that morning.

After they turned onto the dirt road, Martin stopped and Becky pulled up beside him. She lowered her window, and Martin put down the passenger window of the truck.

"Drive ahead," Martin said. "You need to be in front at the clearing so we can unload."

Becky drove her car slowly down the dirt track, Martin's pickup fifty yards behind. The clearing appeared after a couple of minutes, the blue Volvo still inserted in its spot between a couple of trees. Martin seemed to be lagging a little behind. Her eyes on the side mirror, Becky slid down her window and shut off the ignition to wait.

Thirty seconds later Martin's pickup came into view in the mirror. Close behind, a beige and brown sedan followed. When the two vehicles neared her car, Becky saw to her horror that the other car was a deputy sheriff's vehicle. The pickup and the sheriff's sedan stopped and the deputy turned on his blue lights. Becky put her head down on the steering wheel and said a prayer.

Martin led the deputy up to the driver's door of the Camry. "Here she is, officer," Martin was saying. Becky looked up. "I don't understand it," he said. "She just seemed to snap when the police officer arrived."

The deputy nodded. "Step out of the car, ma'am," he said. "You're under arrest."

###

THE CREDIT MANAGER

Since Harry had lost his job two months ago,

he'd been in the habit of getting up early every morning

and starting a pot of coffee before he got dressed. He'd

puttered around in the kitchen all his adult life, but

breakfast had become an obsession with him.

He'd learned to make eggs Benedict, poached

salmon with sherried eggs, muffins filled with fresh

blueberries, fresh croissants and strawberries with cream.

Every morning at 6:30 he'd bring a cup of coffee to

Annie, still sleeping, and wake her by shaking her shoulder.

Annie was an executive secretary at a stock brokerage firm. She had to be downtown by eight.

Harry read the morning paper on his iPad while they ate breakfast. He usually headed straight for the job postings so he could start making phone calls around nine.

"Anything look promising today?" Annie asked. It was just something she always said, part of the routine.

"A couple of things," Harry said. "Actually, one looks pretty good. Southern American is advertising for a credit manager with two years' experience."

Harry looked up. "It's unusual to see a bank job advertised."

"That's you, Harry. Go for it," Annie said. "I'll put these things away while you finish with the listings. I have to go soon."

The first week he'd been out of work, he hadn't felt bad. They had some savings, Harry had answered a couple of ads and finished a project in the townhouse, painting the upstairs rooms.

"You'll be working again soon, Harry," Annie had said the night he'd told her. "You've always been lucky." And later, after they'd had a few drinks, she'd added thoughtfully, "Maybe I could help. I mean, if you don't mind. I can listen out, ask around. A lot of businessmen come into the office. Bankers too, sometimes. Maybe the brokers will know about something."

"Sure. Whatever." Harry had raised his glass in a salute. Harry had watched his wife surreptitiously. She had long dark hair with a natural wave. She wore it pulled back most of the time, in a cascade past her shoulders and down her back. She was tall; she had long legs, dancer's legs; to him, she was beautiful.

Annie finished putting the breakfast things in the dishwasher and came back into the dining room. "I've got to go now," she said. "I want to get to work a little early. We've got auditors coming. Good luck today. Kiss me bye." She bent to kiss him. "See you this afternoon," she said.

"Take care," said Harry.

Harry got up from the table and carried the iPad into the living room. He'd learned, when he was working, to make calls for appointments early, before secretaries arrived, when phones were answered by the people you wanted to speak to. This morning it took five minutes to make an appointment with a vice-president of Southern American for 4:00 that afternoon.

Harry put down the phone and smiled. This could work out.

He had time to read the local paper and the *New York Times*. He liked to read every word, the editorials, the obituaries, business section. The habit had done him a lot of good in the loan business. If a used car dealership was running three-hundred dollar ads in the local paper three days a week, it could afford to pay its debts. Later in the morning, he'd do some chores.

The Taggarts had been planning to buy a washer and dryer, their first, when Harry lost his job. Twice a week, he hoisted their bulky laundry bags to his shoulders, lugging them a hundred yards to the laundromat on the ground floor of the complex's clubhouse. He had a load to do before lunch.

In the work room behind the kitchen, the room that should have been the laundry room, Harry sorted the dirty clothes, shirts, pants, socks going into one bag, delicate items into another. He locked the door of the apartment carefully and started for the laundry, glancing up toward the revolving time and temperature sign on the roof of the First National Bank building across the river. At 10:03, it was seventy-eight degrees. And twenty-one Celsius.

Only one other person was in the laundromat, a man who sat in a plastic chair next to the row of dryers, his face partially hidden by the newspaper he was reading. Harry selected two washing machines and loaded his wash. He placed quarters and dimes in the slots and slammed in both chrome plungers; the machines hissed as they began to fill with water.

Harry stepped outside. He leaned against the brick wall of the clubhouse and gazed out over the pool toward the tennis court. The court was empty at this hour, but a few morning sunbathers with their towels, smart phones, magazines, and soft drink cans had staked out territory around the pool. It was a tiny pool, too small for an adult to do anything except glide the few feet from one end to the other, but it was surrounded by a huge deck of gray concrete.

"I see you're wearing running shoes."

Harry looked around. The man he'd seen in the laundromat stood in the doorway, a touch of amusement on his face. He was short and thin, with blond hair and thick white eyebrows. "Pardon?" Harry said.

"I said I see you're wearing running shoes."

"What? Oh. Yeah. Right. Gotta stay in shape. You know." He shrugged.

"You do a lot of running?" the man asked.

"Yeah. A little. Up and down. I jog."

After he'd lost his job, Harry had begun jogging a few laps around the apartment complex some mornings after Annie left for work.

"Those are pretty good shoes, but they're not as good as mine. The ones I sell," the man added, following Harry's glance at his brown oxfords. He pulled something out of a shirt pocket. "Here," he said. "My card."

Harry looked at the small beige card engraved with the name of a popular running shoe.

"That's me," the man said, pointing. "I'm Joe Siebert." He held out his hand.   Harry still looked down at the card as though he were having trouble making out. the words.

"What? Oh. Hi." They shook hands. "Harry Taggart."

"How you doing, Harry?" Siebert said.

"I'm all right."

"So what line are you in?"

"Credit." Harry spoke quickly. "I'm a credit manager."

"That right? You're in business, too. I like my job. I set my own hours, I make some money. I'm the wholesaler for three states. I average a couple grand a week."

"That's good money," Harry said.

"Yeah, well, it's a lot of travel, hard work, but I can't complain." Siebert looked again at Harry's shoes. They were only a few months old, but already one shoe had a small hole in the toe, through which Harry's toenail showed. He had bought the shoes at a discount store. Harry moved his feet uncomfortably.

"You really do much jogging? I can maybe get you a deal on some shoes. I keep a few pairs in the back of my car, you know, just for friends."

"Well, I don't know."

"Sure, you think about it. I've gotta go make some phone calls. I'm over in 812." He reached out to shake Harry's hand again. "See you around, huh?"

Back in the apartment, Harry turned on the television set and put an egg on to boil for lunch. He usually watched an hour of daytime TV -- two soaps Annie wanted him to record and follow -- but there didn't seem any harm in watching a few minutes of CNN and Weather Channel while the egg cooked.

He took a beer out of the refrigerator on his way back to the living room. The Pope was touring Africa, where, Harry learned, Roman Catholic priests routinely kept concubines.

Harry pulled the tab off the can and took a swallow. There were forest fires in California. He set his beer on an end table and slid off the sofa to the floor, hooked his toes under the front of the love seat across the room, and began doing sit-ups. He kept his head turned toward the TV screen and watched the crawler roll the current stock quotations.

"Credit manager, credit manager," ran through his head to the rhythm of his movements. Credit manager. Hardly a day had passed since the third week in March without those words running through his mind like a line from a bad song. Harry had been credit manager at the Farmers and Merchants Savings and Loan on Fifteenth street for almost two years, and he'd been doing a good job. He'd improved collections on bad loans by fifteen per cent. Of course, the credit manager before Harry had been a gambler and a drunk, and Mr. Warren, his boss, had thought anyone who stayed sober through day would have been an improvement.

Still, he'd been hard-working and conscientious, and he'd done as well as anyone could with a recession on. Maybe he could have been a little tougher, leaned on the slow pays a little harder, but the fast repo just wasn't Harry's style. As soon as he'd walked into Mr. Warren's corner office that afternoon, Harry had known what was coming. It hung in the air of the room like the odor of something dead.

"Harry, sit down," Warren had said.

Harry sat in one of the leather armchairs. Warren remained standing, leaning on the back of the other chair, his eyes moving about the room as though he weren't sure they were alone.

"You know, Harry, it's been tough for you. Harry," Warren had said, "it's this way. Higher management wants to bring in some new people in preparation for the move into our new facility in the mall, and, well, Harry, you're one of the ones being replaced."

"Replaced?" Warren came around the chair, smiling as if he'd just recommended Harry for promotion. "I don't like doing this, believe me. You're a nice guy, Harry. It takes a mean son of' a bitch to run a credit department." He held out his hand. "Good luck, Harry."

Harry accepted the handshake and mumbled, "Thanks, Mr. Warren."

Harry hadn't gone straight home. He'd walked around town for awhile, hardly noticing the store windows and shoppers and traffic and other men dressed in business suits. He went clear through the business district and ended up on the University campus at the edge of town.

There, he strayed from the sidewalks and crossed half a dozen quadrangles, each with its green grass and oak trees, surrounded by brick and stone buildings fronted by columns.

Harry had been a student at the University not long ago. He recognized no one, and even the buildings seemed different from how he remembered. It was like the feeling he'd had as a college senior when, thinking of enrolling in graduate school, he'd traveled to a dozen campuses in half a dozen states and found that each one, though slightly different from the rest, seemed so familiar to him that he felt he'd never really left his old school. It was this impression that had made him decide it was time for a taste of the real world.

When he reached the far edge of the campus, he doubled back and walked down University Boulevard toward the Strip, a couple of blocks of bookstores, delis, record shops, diners, beer bars, and pizzerias. There was a movie theatre on the corner. The walk and the smells of food in the air had made Harry hungry. Across from the theatre, there had been a diner when he was in school. The Kwik Snak. It had been Harry's regular place for breakfast. The building was still there, but now it was called Steak & Egg Kitchen.

Harry went in and chose a booth under the window at the front. He looked over at the counterman, who signaled to a waitress without pausing from wiping the counter with a wet gray cloth. Harry noticed that the man had one cauliflower ear, purple and knotted. He wondered if the man had been a boxer.

The waitress came over with her pad and a stubby pencil. Harry ordered a grilled cheese, French fries and a Coke. When she brought the food, he ate as though he'd been without a meal for days.

While he chewed, Harry looked out the window and watched the traffic, students riding bicycles or walking. Many wore backpacks of bright nylon, orange, yellow, electric blue. Across the street at the movie theater, he could just make out a sign that read Econo Hour 3:30. There was a poster taped to the plate glass window of the theatre. The poster looked blank.

Harry checked his watch. He might see a movie. He left a dollar for the waitress, picked up the check, and headed for the cash register.

The counterman put down his cloth and came over. "Did you work here when the place was called Kwik Snak?" Harry asked.

The man turned his good ear at a better angle and handed Harry his change. "Called what?"

"Kwik Snak. It used to be called Kwik Snak," Harry said. "You don't remember?"

"Sure don't, mister. Always been the Steak & Egg since I been here."

Harry weighed the change in his palm, unsatisfied. "It used to be called Kwik Snak."

"I don't doubt what you're saying," said the man, picking up his rag and returning to his place at the counter. "I just said I don't remember it."

Harry nodded slowly. "Well. Have a nice day," he said.

"Sure, you too," the counterman said.

Outside, Harry crossed the street to find out what was playing at the theatre. The poster he'd thought was blank was in black and white; the only image was the head of a deer in the center. Harry looked at his watch, glanced down the street at the First National sign; on top of the twentieth floor, it could be seen from anywhere in town. Both read 3:21.

Harry went up to the ticket window and bought a ticket. Just inside the door, he handed the ticket to an usher who wore a red double-breasted jacket with gold piping and two rows of buttons down the front.

In the cool theatre lobby, Harry leaned against a wall to wait for the early show to end. It was a twin theatre; he could hear, faintly, the sound tracks of both shows.

Harry held himself erect, every vertebra flat against the block wall. He felt a slight chill creep down his legs. Without turning his head, Harry could see the entire lobby. He watched a short gray-haired woman push through the door without stopping at the box office. She walked up to the usher and showed him a card. He shook his head but allowed her to come in. Once inside, she paused to make a survey of the lobby, her head swinging slowly from side to side.

When the woman spotted Harry, she began to walk toward him, moving hesitantly at first, then faster and faster, as though she thought he might disappear before she could get to him.

The woman stopped dead in front of him. There was a faint odor of stale tobacco on her breath. She handed Harry the same card she'd shown the usher.

Harry stared at the woman, waiting for her to speak. She motioned to the card. He looked at it. It was made of cheap white paper and printed with smudgy black ink. I AM A DEAF PERSON, the card said.

Harry looked up from the card. He kept his eyes straight ahead, his spine pressed against the cool wall. "Go to hell," he said.

Comfortable in a red plush seat inside the theatre, Harry thought maybe he'd go back to the bank when the movie was over and tell Mr. Warren what he'd done. Warren would see that Harry had what it takes and would be glad to hire him back, a fire-eater like that. But then Harry remembered that Warren had been just following orders and couldn't hire him back even if he wanted to.

Harry watched the movie, but he paid little attention to the plot. Later, he would remember few details. He couldn't tell Annie its name. He recalled only one thing clearly, that one character, one human character, had looked very much like the deer he'd seen on the poster, and that the character had looked more and more like a deer as the film went on. That was the name he'd finally given Annie for the movie when she'd pressed -- The Deer.

When the lights came up, Harry rushed out of the theatre. If she were still in the area, he wanted to find the deaf woman and apologize. He'd never done anything like that in this life, unless you counted that one time when he was a kid, walking down the street with his parents and stopping to pluck a pack of chewing gum out of the fingers of a blind man who sold pencils and gum on the sidewalk. The man had been holding out the gum as though he were offering it to Harry, and Harry had taken it right out of his hand. People were always giving chewing gum to kids in those days, before everybody knew it rotted your teeth. Until today Harry had never been able to pass a beggar on the street without reaching into his pocket for change.

Harry pushed through the crowd and hit the sidewalk. The old lady had finished working the theater and was approaching the street corner. He raced after her and skidded around the corner, just in time to see her swing into the front seat of a shiny silver Cadillac and drive away. "I'll be damned," Harry said.

He walked slowly back around the corner, breathing hard, his hands by his sides. Far down the street, he could see the towering First National Bank building with its green number 1 and its revolving time and temperature sign. At 5:41, it was sixty-seven degrees.

Harry felt sick. He stumbled back into the theatre lobpy. In the men's room, he found an unoccupied stall, latched the door, and sat down. He laced his fingers across his face and wept.

Harry poured hot water out of the boiler he'd used to cook his egg and replaced it with water from the COLD tap. He cracked the egg against the metal rim of the boiler and gingerly picked off bits of shell, constantly turning the egg to keep from burning his fingers.

He'd learned to cook a few things besides breakfast since he'd lost his job, stuffed flounder, Coquilles St. Jacques, some New Orleans dishes. He made a good shrimp Creole. The trade school had advertised a Chinese cooking course that he'd wanted to take, but it cost too much.

He mashed the egg with chopped pickles and a few bits of celery from a stalk he'd found in the hydrator and spread the mixture on a slice of rye bread. He ate his sandwich and finished his beer in the living room while he watched the mid-day news.

The Headline News channel had already covered everything. Harry wiped out his plate and put it in the dishwasher. On the credenza that supported the Samsung monitor, he found quarters for the dryers. He jogged down to the laundromat.

The pool deck was beginning to fill with sunbathers now; on the tennis court, a couple of college girls were playing a slow game. Harry pulled his wet clothes, smelling of soap and chlorine, out of the washers. He carried them by hand, four double handfuls, across the room and stuffed them into a couple of machines.

Trotting back to the apartment, Harry felt a surge of energy. Inside, he raced upstairs to search for the swimming trunks he'd bought last year when he'd been in Tampa for a credit managers' conference. He found the trunks in the back of a dresser drawer, stripped off his clothes and pulled them on. He examined himself in the full length mirror on the back of the closet door. Not bad. Really not so very bad at all. He raised his arms and flexed his stomach muscles.

There was still a fine line of definition down his middle. He marked it off with a finger. Almost in shape.

Back downstairs, Harry reached for the remote. It was time to record Annie's soaps. Starting the recording had become a daily ritual, though he could have programmed the DVR to record automatically. But today his hand stopped in midair. He could skip a day.

He stood straight. It was as though he'd just realized this fact. It seemed momentous. He could skip a day. Annie could watch the programs a few days later on the network websites if she wanted. The cable had a soaps rerun channel too. Annie hardly asked about the programs and didn't always watch them. What she usually asked about, first thing, was the interviews.

The interview today was the first he'd been able to line up at a bank. There wasn't usually much turnover in banking. People got a job and stayed put.

Harry sat on the carpeted floor and did ten minutes of yoga, stretching exercises designed to improve the muscle tone of the legs. He hooked his bare toes under the love seat and knocked off forty sit-ups as fast as he could, knees bent, hands behind his head. He finished the last ·dozen in perfect rhythm without slowing, flipped over and did twenty pushups. Then he stood and ran back upstairs, taking the steps two at a time.

Harry tucked the laundry basket under an arm and rapped sharply on the door of apartment 812. After a moment, the door opened slightly, and one of Joseph Siebert's eyes appeared.

"Yeah?"

"Hello, Siebert. Listen, I want to see those running shoes."

"What?"

"You said you had some running shoes to sell."

The eye blinked once and then widened. The door opened.

"Sure, Harry, come on in, have a seat. Can't pass up a deal like that, right?"   "Maybe not. Let's see the shoes."

"Okay," Siebert said. "They're out in my car."

The space behind the seats of Joe Siebert's white Corvette was piled high with boxes of running shoes in several sizes and models. Harry bought three pairs -- two for himself, a training model and a light, flexible racer's pair, and one for his wife, who had never shown the slightest interest in jogging.

Harry paid Siebert with a check, stacked his boxes of shoes in the laundry basket, and set out for his final trip to the laundromat. On the way, he glanced once at the bank sign across the river. 12:26. Plenty of time before the interview.

Both loads of clothes were dry. Harry tossed everything into the laundry basket and hurried back to the apartment. He'd dropped the basket on the living room floor and took his new training shoes out of their box. They smelled of fresh glue and rubber.

In the bottom of the box, he found a pamphlet. Congratulations, it said. You have just purchased a pair of the finest running shoes in the world. Underneath these words was a monochrome print of a runner rampant against a stylized city skyline, his shorts billowing around his thighs, the muscles in his legs finely detailed. Puffy clouds pushed up from the horizon beyond the skyline. One shoe, greatly exaggerated in size, was flexed to show the tread pattern.

Harry picked up one of the shoes and turned it over. Each little knob of the tread reminded him of a miniature baseball diamond with four knobs of its own at each corner, smaller than pinheads, for the bases.

Harry turned the shoe and began to lace it. His fingers felt clumsy, the lacing complicated. There was a diagram to explain the system; it took ten minutes to lace both shoes.

Harry stood and flexed his toes. He ran in place for a couple of minutes to warm up, then stepped outside and locked the door. He pushed the apartment key to the bottom of the tiny pocket on his swimming trunks.

Jogging toward the highway, Harry met Siebert, struggling with a laundry basket full of neatly folded towels. "Better get that laundry done, sport," Siebert said.

Harry smiled as he jogged past. "Go to hell, Siebert," he said.

The new shoes were light and soft. Harry had the sensation that he was floating, just skimming the surface of the asphalt. He held his head high and flew down the road.

Before he entered a stretch of roadway shaded by huge oak and maple trees, Harry glimpsed, across the river, the First National Bank sign. He couldn't read the temperature, but the shade was cool. Harry ran faster, breathing easily to the rhythm of his legs.

The Southern American Bank's main office was on the edge of downtown, across the street from the downtown Ramada. At five minutes to four, Harry was seated on a brown leather sofa in the reception area of the commercial loan department on the third floor, waiting to see Richard O'Mary, vice-president of commercial loans.

A blonde receptionist about twenty years old, wearing a skirt with side slits, had taken his resume in to O'Mary when he'd come in. Harry held the lobby copy of *Barron's* open on his legs, pretending to read an article on interest rates and the Fed.

Harry was a heavy sweater. About three o'clock, he had showered and shaved and put on a starched white shirt with a red and blue regimental-stripe tie and gray suit, as near as he had to banker's clothes. He had trouble staying dry after his shower, even though he had turned down the air conditioning in the apartment. Even now, a trickle of sweat had started between his shoulder blades and was working its way down his spine.

The door to the office behind the receptionist's desk opened, and a man emerged. Smiling, he walked toward Harry with his hand extended.

Harry stood. "Harry Taggart?" the man said. "I'm Richard O'Mary. Good to see you."

"It's nice to meet you, Richard," Harry said.

"Come on into my office."

Harry followed O'Mary into a paneled office with glass-enclosed bookcases along one wall. O'Mary gestured toward one of the chairs in front of an oak desk. Harry moved it half an inch before settling in. He felt good. He knew how to interview.

O'Mary asked about his college background, his experience. He spent less time than Harry had feared on his being fired. "It happens," O'Mary said. "Sometimes it's nobody's fault. I've been fired, once. Good people use it as an opportunity." He leaned forward and planted his elbows on the desk. "Mr. Taggart, we're interviewing five men for this position. You're the third. I can tell you now that you're the best qualified. We've got two more interviews this week." He stood and came around the desk to shake Harry's hand. "I like the way you handle yourself, Harry. We're obligated to those interviews, but on Friday afternoon, I'd stay near the phone if I were you." He moved to open the door. "Thanks for coming in, Harry."

Harry walked quickly from the bank lobby toward his car. It was only about fifty feet, but his shirt was sticky with sweat by the time he reached the curb. It was hot, but there was a storm building, a thundercloud pushing its dark mass high over the western edge of town. Maybe tonight it would rain and break the heat. Annie would be home by five-thirty. He wanted to stop by The Decanter and buy a bottle of Taittinger on the way home. This interview was worth celebrating.

Annie came in at five-forty. Harry told her the news while he prepared dinner. Most of it was already done. In twenty minutes, they were sitting down to stuffed flounder, asparagus, French bread, and Champagne.

There was thunder in the distance, a continuous drum roll. It would rain soon. They finished the champagne reclining in the floor of the living room, Annie with her dancer's legs crossed at the ankles, Harry supporting himself with one elbow on the sofa. Harry made a toast with his last swallow of wine.

"To the Southern American Bank," he said. "To Harry and Annie," said Annie. Upstairs, they got undressed in a hurry. Harry went into the bathroom to brush his teeth and rinse out the taste of wine and fish, while Annie got her diaphragm out of the drawer in her bedside table.

Harry hated to watch her insert the thing. It looked medical. He hated all that stuff. Maybe they'd have a kid, now that it looked like he'd be back at work.

In bed, Annie had the sheet over her. He pulled it aside and kissed her and began to touch her breasts. They were both a little drunk, but he was all right. Yes. It was all right.

Afterwards, Harry was about to drift off to sleep when he felt Annie get up and pad into the bathroom. He heard the toilet flush. He lay on his back looking at the ceiling, not thinking much of anything. Then she was back beside him, an arm flung over his chest. He noticed his shoulder was damp.

"Hey," he said. "You okay?"

"Yeah," she sniffed. "I'm all right. Harry," she said. "I need to tell you something. It's a thing you have to know, that I have to tell you, it's, I don't know."

"What?" He looked at her, raising one shoulder. "What is it?"

"You remember, Harry, when you lost your job, I said I'd listen around the office, you know, ask around and try to help?

"Sure. I remember. So?"

"So, I did. One of the men from Southern American Bank, an executive V.P., he comes in a lot, he manages the bank's bond portfolio, futures trading, hedges, that kind of stuff."

Harry raised himself onto one elbow and began tracing the margin of his wife's thigh with a finger. She took his hand and held it still.

"Right. Anyway, one of the brokers who handles the account, Tom Overmyer, he mentioned to this guy that you were looking for something. Well anyway, this guy, he's a real toad, short, a little fat, blond hair but thin on top. I think his family owns a lot of stock in the bank."

Harry freed his hand and began to stroke her thigh again. "So he talked to you about a job for me."

"He asked me out for a drink."

"Oh. "

"A business drink after work. You know. We went to McQueen's. We had a couple of drinks, talking about the investment business, and then he started saying things, like if I'd be nice to him, he could see about getting you a job."

Harry's hand stopped. "And you told him where to go."

"Well, I was shocked. I mean, it sounds naive, nothing like that ever happened to me. I told him no way, Jose."

Harry resumed his stroking. "What's this guy's name?"

"It's a funny name. O'Mary."

"Richard O'Mary."

"Yes. That's the one."

"I see."

"I forgot about it after a few days. But then, it had been a month, nothing, you were getting depressed, we were both miserable, Harry, and one day during break, I went to the phone booth on the corner, and I called him. Harry," she said, and he could feel his chest damp again, "Harry, one day a couple of weeks ago I went to a hotel with him during lunch, and I went to bed with him. I didn't want it, Harry, I just, you were out of work, and we needed stuff, and, I don't know. I mean, just once, I thought maybe we'd get something out of the bastards."

He didn't feel the way he'd have thought he would. He didn't feel much of anything. Truth was, right now, it felt like maybe it didn't matter. He needed a drink of water. He got out of bed and went into the bathroom and poured some water into a bathroom glass.

The rain had finally come; it pinged against the window. There was a high wind. Out of the corner of his eye he saw his wife coming toward him, naked, her eyes red, her arms outstretched. Her mouth was open. She seemed to be saying something Harry couldn't hear.

He turned quickly and something fell off the lavatory. Trying to catch it, he couldn't seem to move as fast as usual. He couldn't tell why. He knew he wasn't drunk. He knocked over some other things. It didn't seem to matter.

# # #

A SUMMER DREAM

Arthur Lybrand stopped at Kroger on his way home from work to pick up a few things his wife had asked him to get for the weekend. They liked to cook something special on Saturday nights. It was a Friday in late summer. Arthur hurried across the blistering asphalt parking lot, but in the cold supermarket air he dawdled.

He pushed his shopping cart needlessly down every aisle, here following a tan girl wearing cut-offs and bikini top, there pausing to admire the selection of imported bottled waters. He picked up fresh mushrooms from Produce, two small speckled trout in Seafood, a package of slivered almonds, a can of black cherries for a flaming dessert. He'd chosen a domestic white wine and was on his way to Express Checkout when he caught a scent -- an aroma -- on the air, somewhere between Gourmet Foods and Cookies and Crackers. It was a man's cologne, a fat, balding man in golf shirt and plaid Bermuda shorts, though it could have been the tall thin black man in the business suit, or maybe both. Arthur couldn't be sure.

He pushed his cart into line and looked around. In front of him a young Asian woman was piling an amazing number of honeydew melons on the checker's conveyer belt.

He didn't know the brand of the fragrance. But as he caught one more whiff of whatever it was on that sweltering summer day in the cool of Kroger's air conditioning, he was instantly transported into a fantasy world far more real than the supermarket.

It was a crisp November night. The air had that brittle, pristine clarity of late autumn nights when the temperature has dropped below thirty-two degrees and Cassiopeia seems no more than an arm's length away.

Arthur was with his wife. They were in the middle of a throng of people stirring about with no distinct purpose in mind, though they were all moving slowly in the same direction. He did notice that all the women were naked. His vision began to swirl.

When it settled, he was seated in the football stadium of the state university from which both he and his wife had graduated. Their seats were among the best, near the fifty-yard line. Around them sat expansive, established upper-middle class alumni, the men and women all dressed as though they had cocktail parties to attend soon after the game. The mingled odors of autumn, bourbon whiskey, and blood lust hung in the air, laced sharply with the bite of a particular men's cologne. It seemed to be the only scent the men were wearing. Out on the field the home team was going about its usual work of wearing down the opposition.

Arthur managed to stumble through the checkout line in the midst of this reverie and somehow made his way outside. He came to his senses crossing the scalding parking lot on the way to his car, just in time to avoid being run over by a tiny gray-haired lady driving a Buick sedan the size of Fort Knox, who shook her fist menacingly as she thundered past.

Her reaction was quite normal under the circumstances, Arthur supposed. The heat has upset the function of her hypothalamus enough to cause such irrational bursts of anger. Medicine was an interest of Arthur's.

He got in his car and started home toward East River, toward his five-bedroom house with its super view of the golf course, toward Margie, his wife, and their two daughters. Toward central air-conditioning.

Arthur's car, with its Moroccan leather interior and inadequate air flow, was as hot as the Arabian desert at noon. The stench of all that hot leather, that heady aroma so touted in glossy magazine advertising, was stifling. But in spite of the heat that shimmered off the highway and turned patches of asphalt into sticky goo, there was, somehow, a hint of autumn in the air.

And suddenly it was there again. Or rather, there Arthur was again, seated in the crisp of a football night with his wife and friends from the neighborhood, other corporate vice-presidents, doctors, stockbrokers, their wives. No mistresses were present. Arthur belonged to a conservative group.

Arthur ignored his friends, his attention focused a few rows down from he sat where a woman sat, a woman with whom Arthur had fallen immediately and deeply in love. He couldn't have said precisely why. It was the effect she created. She had dark hair with tints of red, worn longer than the popular style, falling in soft curls about her shoulders. Her suit was a fairly modish wool, and she wore a small rimless hat, almost a beret, pulled low over one ear. And her

face. There was something vaguely familiar about that face.

Arthur sat behind her, but also at an acute angle, so that he could see the curve of her jaw, one pretty little ear, at times a near profile when she turned her head to observe some play on the field or to hear some remark made by a friend. It was the most serene, reposed, haunting face he had ever seen or imagined, even though Arthur was of the upper-middle class Southern caste accustomed to female beauty. The woman of his vision was a modern goddess.

Later, Arthur couldn't remember how the accident happened. His attention had wandered. He felt a sharp jolt that snapped his head forward and back. He had smashed into the car in front of him, stopped for a traffic light.

He rushed out to make sure no one was hurt. He apologized to the young couple in the other car to the point of making himself a nuisance.

"It's okay," the young man said.

They exchanged addresses and insurance agents while the woman called the local police on her cell phone.

Arthur turned over his agent's card and saw that he had already violated a cardinal rule from a list of "Things to Do After an Accident" on the back: *Number 1. Never mention the subject of fault until the arrival of authorities. Though you may think you are clearly at fault, you may not be aware of all the facts.*

By the time he had finished reading the card, a police car had rolled up and two policemen were climbing out.

Arthur stared. Both men were blond, blue-eyed, six feet two, with matching dimples, cleft chins and bushy eyebrows. The city must have been running off cops on a secret invention by Xerox, Arthur thought.

No one else seemed to notice. Maybe the invention wasn't secret. Maybe he had just fallen asleep watching CNN and missed the announcement.

They were nice fellows, these xeroxed cops. They spoke in complete sentences, their grammar was perfect, and Arthur liked them even though they gave him a ticket and a lecture on inattention. They were impressed with Arthur's car. One (or both--Arthur wasn't sure of this) kept asking how much repairing one of these things cost.

The twin officers handled the accident report quickly, and Arthur was on his way again in half an hour, his car's nose smashed, the interior smelling of fish.

Pulling into his drive at last, Arthur felt barely able to slink toward the door. He needed a drink, he needed his family, he needed the comforts of home. Inside, he announced that he was home.

There was no answer. He took the groceries into the kitchen and called first for Margie, then for Kim and Susan. He put the food in the refrigerator, stepped into the den, and opened the curtains in front of the sliding glass door that looked out over the golf course. Wide green fairways, emerald greens, massive oaks. But not a human being in sight. He turned away from the window and started down the hall toward the bedrooms. He could hear water splashing, muffled squeals. He walked faster.

"Aha" he said. "Life. Family. I've found you." He burst into the children's bathroom, expecting to find Margie giving the girls their baths.

Instead he found the enormous rear of a middle-aged black woman. She kneeled over the rim of the tub, soaping the glowing pink skin of his daughters. He guessed she was the maid, since she wore a maid's uniform. This was fortunate, because Arthur had never seen her before.

"Hi, Daddy!" the girls screamed. "Hello, girls," he said. "Aren't you glad Daddy's home?" Arthur had decided long ago never to be abashed at anything he did or said before the help, an act of considerable courage, because he'd grown up in the northern part of the state, in the hill country, where nobody had maid service. For years after Margie and he were married he'd hardly spoken in the presence of a maid until Margie had begun to worry that they weren't communicating, and Arthur had had to explain.

The maid didn't get up, but twisted her neck around to speak. "I'm Agatha," she said. "The new nanny."

"So I see," said Arthur. "Where's my wife, Agatha?"

"Oh. Mrs. Lybrand. She had to go to market to buy some steaks. She should be home anytime. I believe she said you're having company for dinner."

"Damn. Margie." Arthur thought he said it under his breath, but Agatha gave him a look of reproach.

"Are you all right. Daddy?" asked Susan, the oldest. "Daddy's all right honey," he said. "Daddy worked hard, and he's tired, and he had a wreck coming home, and he could use a drink, and he hoped to rest tonight with his family, but Daddy's all right. Have your bath now."

Arthur turned around and closed the door behind him. In the den he poured three fingers of Johnny Walker Red from a new bottle into a tumbler and collapsed on the sofa. He had just started to enjoy feeling sorry for himself, a repressed alcoholic Southerner who sees visions that cause automobile accidents and who, on top of it all, can't stand the taste of Bourbon whisky, when he heard Margie come through the garage door into the kitchen.

Drink in hand, Arthur hoisted himself up and crossed the room. Margie was unloading sacks full of steaks, potatoes, and two kinds of lettuce.

"Hi," said Arthur. "What happened to Dorothy?" Dorothy was their old maid, one whom he'd just begun to be able to ignore; new help still required major adjustments in his personality.

"Dorothy is gone," Margie said.

"Why?"

Margie was crossing the kitchen with an armload of salad greens. "The story I told the agency -- and the girls -- was that I caught her watering the Scotch. They hear that enough to believe it, or at least to pretend to. The truth is that when I came in from my run this morning she was screwing one of the golf course maintenance men on the living room floor."

Arthur swallowed a mouthful of Scotch. "Good Christ," he said. "So you fired her."

"So I fired her."

"Well. Dorothy. Uhh, what's this nonsense about a dinner party?

"I don't know about any nonsense about a dinner party. But you need to go out and start the charcoal. We're grilling steaks for the Adamsons and the Stuarts. They'll be here at six."

Stuarts? Adamsons? "Do we know these people?" Arthur asked. "Do you know how hot it is outside?"

"I know them from the agency. Nadine Adamson and Liz Stuart. I told them to bring their husbands. I was sure you wouldn't mind."

About a year earlier Margie had started back to work as a real estate agent, to help expand her outlook, she'd said. In her first two months she'd sold four houses and made more money then Arthur make in three.

He tried a different tack. "I had a wreck on the way home," he said.

"I don't have time for your stories," she said. "Save it for dinner. Right now I've got to freshen up while you start the steaks. Everybody grills out these days. It's less work." She brushed past him out of the kitchen, stopping for a second to sample my Scotch. "That's good." she said. "Make me one of those while I change. Sweetheart."

Arthur could think of nothing to say as he watched his wife leave the room. He took off his coat and tie, rolled up his sleeves, stepped onto the patio, and began to sweat. He opened the storage room and took out a bag of charcoal. He started mounding charcoal briquets on the grill. The outdoor thermometer one of the girls had given him for a birthday present registered 98. He wished he hadn't looked.

What Margie had said about cooking out was true. All around, from backyard pits, grills, smokers, braziers, hibachiis, wisps of smoke trailed into the air. The husbands of the neighborhood, drunken, vainglorious, captive, were cooking dinner. Squint a little and the suburbs looked like the siege of Richmond. If there had even been a siege of Richmond.

The dinner party was predictable -- too long, too serious, too drunken. The women talked real estate as though they, and not a supreme being, had invented it, and their husbands vied with each other for boorish-lout-of-the-year honors.

Fortunately it was cut short just before the Cherries Jubilee by a peep from the emergency beeper in

Dr. Norman Adamson's breast pocket, though what the emergency could have been, or why an ear, nose, and throat man should even need the device, was never explained to Arthur's satisfaction.

When they had all gone, he tried again to tell Margie about the accident. He'd decided to save a tale so worth telling for when they were alone. He'd wanted to bore his dinner guests as much as possible so that next time Margie invited them they would manufacture plausible but socially-acceptable excuses like "My father is ill," or "We just learned the children have body lice," or "Poor Norman has discovered his mistress is a lesbian."

"Margie, honey," he began as they were doing the dishes. "I tried to tell you this earlier, but I had the oddest experience today." He'd decided to throw caution to the winds and tell her the whole story in the hope of gaining a little sympathy and saving himself a visit to the company shrink.

"I hoped there was some explanation for your behavior at dinner," she said.

"What do you mean, 'my behavior'?"

She stopped washing a steak platter long enough to set her chin and kindle a flare in her eye. "I mean: your inattention to conversation, your insistence on discussing hunger in Africa just as we began the steaks, your belittling Norm Adamson's medical practice as though you were some great big success story -- do you know he cleared over a quarter of a million dollars last year 'swabbing sore throats' as you put it? Which he had the grace not to point out. And finally--

finally -- saying to Nadine, who I seated next to you at the dinner table because I thought you would like her, her. . . ."

"Conversation topics?"

"....boobs, saying to her, 'that's as well-matched a string of imitation pearls as I've seen in a while.'"

"Well, they were. Norman probably paid almost as much as he would've for the real thing."

"I'm surprised you didn't ask to rub them against your teeth."

"Maybe next time."

"As though you could afford real pearls, of course. Sometimes I wonder what happened to that super-achiever KA president I married."

This had always been a little social exaggeration of Margie's. Arthur had only been vice president of his chapter. He decided it wasn't the time to point out the discrepancy.

"What's the matter with you lately anyway? You never go to the club anymore. Dee Harrison was saying just the other day at their swim party that he hadn't seen you on the course in ages. Have you lost your ambition?"

An image of Dee Harrison, martini glass in hand, paunchy gut, exposed, leering down at Margie in her string bikini, almost choked Arthur. "So Dee was there, huh?" he said. "I thought that was a party just for the girls."

"Don't change the subject. How are you ever going to make senior vice-president puttering around the kitchen looking morose or shutting yourself up in the study for hours?"

"I never look morose, Margie. And Tri-States has all the senior veeps it needs for awhile."

"One of these days they just might find they don't need you at all. It's a damn good thing I'm doing so well in real estate. Without my income I swear I think you'd let the girls attend public school."

"Don't gloat, Margie. It doesn't become you."

That did it. With a final, end-of conversation grunt, she flung away from the sink. "I'm going to bed," she said. "And by the way, maybe since you wrecked your precious sports car, you can be persuaded to sell it. We could never afford it in the first place."

Arthur poured himself another drink and went into the girls' room. Susan was still awake, and he knelt beside her bed. "Daddy had a wreck today, Susan," he said. "He's okay though. It's been quite a day."

"I know, Daddy," she said. "You told us already. It's all right though. Why don't you go and get some sleep?"

Arthur walked out of his daughters' room and down the hall to his study. He went in, closed the door and sat at his desk, cradling his drink and rocking slowly in the leather desk chair. He thought again of the girl in his vision, the girl in the little hat at the football stadium. He knew she reminded him of someone. The unconscious rarely conjured up anything really new; the source must have been some memory, buried deeply. His dream girl.

Seventh grade. The high school gym. His parents, civic-minded, innocent, cleaning up after the cakewalk, the musical chairs, the jazz band. Everyone else long gone. A game of hide

and seek. The concrete stage. Dressing rooms, training rooms. The
smells of liniment and sweat and dust.

Arthur opened his eyes and shook his head
sharply. He rose, walked to the window, and stared out
into the darkness of the golf course. He raised the glass
of whisky to his lips and drained it in one long burning
swallow.

Two weeks later the Lybrands received the
obligatory return invitation to the Adamsons'. Arthur
didn't want to go, but Margie could be persuasive. He
soon found his knees tucked under the mahogany table
in Nadine Adamson's formal dining room in an
imitation Georgian mansion in Kingsridge, the new
suburb for the truly arrived, ten miles out from town

and carved out of a bog that had never been much good for anything.

The dinner was one of those where some hired cook has peeled shrimp and crab all morning, where a standing rib roast from the Midwest has taken its first and last airplane ride just for the privilege of being the main course at the Adamsons' dinner party.

Arthur found himself seated across from Nadine, presumably by her choice. He felt the victim of a conspiracy. At least, Nadine wore a conspiratorially low-cut dress, sans imitation pearls this time. The Adamson breasts were large but otherwise unimpressive.

Arthur was polite through dinner. He made no remarks about jewelry. He didn't object when the good doctor entertained the group with his latest ear reconstruction. He made conversation about the new greens at the club and the need for a strong national defense through servings of shrimp saki, French onion soup, crab meat salad, and three wines. During the orange sherbet, he was even able to work himself up to a risqué comment or two to Nadine about the Harrisons' swim party.

After dinner they moved to the music room. Norm Adamson wanted to show off his newest acquisition, a Steinway grand. A piano player had been hired, Norman promised Bach and Chopin.

When Arthur saw the woman seated at the piano, he was speechless. She wore a simple white dress and little makeup, but it was impossible to conceal the fact that she was the only really pretty woman in the house. Her skin was the purest ivory. Her hair was chestnut brown, arranged in a chignon. As she leaned over the keyboard, a few tendrils escaped to trail down the back of her graceful neck. Her carriage, the expression on her face, managed to suggest not that she considered herself above her present station, but outside it, as though this house, the men and women for whom she played, were enclosed in parentheses, isolated from the general drift of things.

Arthur scarcely heard the music. As Brandy Alexanders were served, Arthur asked his host where they'd found her. "The Music Department at the University." he said.

He should have expected that, Arthur thought. None of the other women in the room would have chosen her if she had interviewed her in person; it was too obvious her breeding outclassed theirs. She was beautiful, and beauty, Arthur believed, had nothing to do with rank.

After the hour of music was over, saying good night to the Adamsons, the Stuarts, the Richardsons, the Hemphills, Arthur asked Norm Adamson for the woman's name.

That night, his marriage, which had never been held together, Arthur realized, by much more than the convenience of a fraternity-sorority pledge swap, began a rapid and fatal deterioration. Margie was silent until they were home and the babysitter had gone. "You really did it tonight, didn't you?"

"Did what?"

"You've made a fool of me in front of my friends for the last time. I hate you. I want you out of my life."

Arthur followed her to the bedroom door. "I've certainly never needed you, your hair dye, your dumb, boozy friends. I'm divorcing you, Margie."

She slammed the door. The next day Arthur was at the office and on the phone by six. He couldn't get a response that early so he spent two hours cleaning out his desk. At eight the Music Department answered. "This is Arthur Lybrand," he began. Already his name sounded strange in the quiet office. "I'm -- uhh -- a good friend of Dr. Norman Adamson. Could you, would you be so kind as to look up the name and phone number of the pianist who entertained for him last evening? The music was without equal."

"Certainly, sir, just a moment," said the voice at the Music Department.

Arthur swiveled around in his chair to look out the window while he waited. He could swear that the leaves of the hardwoods in the park across the street were beginning to change color.

The caress of blue velvet curtains. Backstage right, prompter's nook. Now here, truly dark. Nervous laughter. Searching, coming closer.

"Sir?" said the voice. "We're very pleased when our students get

compliments like yours. I assume you'd like her to entertain at your own party? Did you say you'd like that phone number, sir?"

Arthur managed to say yes.

The voice at the music department gave him the number, and he never returned to his wife or to his five-bedroom ranch and its golf course vista and its odors of neighborhood barbecues and adulteries and despair.

In his father's study in rural Connecticut, where the old man moved after retiring and selling his Georgia farm land to Atlanta real-estate developers for what to him seemed a fortune, Arthur Lybrand sits reading. His father's Georgia land now contained condominium apartments and townhouses, and across the road were a country club, a housing development, a golf course. The developer advertised that it was only an hour from downtown Atlanta. There is no Georgia anymore, his father had said, only Atlanta and suburbs.

That visit to Kroger was years ago, and Arthur lives here with his new wife, whose name is Catherine. Arthur's daughters are both in New York, successful career girls, one in advertising, the other on Wall Street.

Catherine sometimes plays Chopin on their one extravagance, a grand piano. Arthur inherited the place three years ago, his father having died here in his adopted home. His father loved the place. There are no lawns, no barbecues--and Arthur sold his car last year after he discovered that it was deteriorating from disuse.

On summer nights sitting out under the big elm, they could strain their eyes for hours without glimpsing a single artificial light. After sitting there under the stars, Catherine wearing a light sweater against the chill, Arthur sitting in silence and smoking the pipe that he discovered among his father's things, they go into their cottage and make love, the cold moonlight pouring in

the windows. sometimes lying awake in each other's

arms through the night and sleeping the next day, and

no voice ever rises on the night to wonder whether one

is richer than the other.

# # #

ABOUT THE AUTHOR

Steven P. Gregory earned B.A., M.F.A., and J.D. degrees from the University of Alabama. Gregory has practiced law since 1991, concentrating on complex litigation and alternative dispute resolution. The stories in *The Dreamer's Mistress and Other Stories* appeared in slightly different form in his M.F.A. thesis, along with other short fiction.

Gregory's first novel, *Cold Winter Rain*, was published in 2013. More information and a link to Gregory's blog can be found at http:// stevenpgregory.com/.

www.ingramcontent.com/pod-product-compliance
Lightning Source LLC
Chambersburg PA
CBHW021047130626
46552CB00005B/2050